Dear mouse friends,
Welcome to the world of

Geronimo Stilton

THE RODENT'S GAZETTE
EDITORIAL STAFF

Geronimo Stilton
A learned and brainy
mouse; editor of
The Rodent's Gazette

Thea Stilton
Geronimo's sister and
special correspondent at
The Rodent's Gazette

Trap Stilton
An awful joker;
Geronimo's cousin and
owner of the store
Cheap Junk for Less

Benjamin Stilton
A sweet and loving
nine-year-old mouse;
Geronimo's favorite
nephew

SUPERSTORE
SURPRISE

Scholastic Inc.

Published by Scholastic Inc., *Publishers since 1920*, 557 Broadway, New York, NY 10012. SCHOLASTIC and associated logos are trademarks and/or registered trademarks of Scholastic Inc.

Stilton is the name of a famous English cheese. It is a registered trademark of the Stilton Cheese Makers' Association.

This book is a work of fiction. Names, characters, places, and incidents are either the product of the author's imagination or are used fictitiously, and any resemblance to actual persons, living or dead, business establishments, events, or locales is entirely coincidental.

ISBN 978-1-338-65499-8

Text by Geronimo Stilton
Original title Grande Mistero al Megastore
Cover by Iacopo Bruno, Roberto Ronchi, and Alessandro Muscillo
Illustrations by Daria Cerchi, Ivan Bigarella, and Valeria Cairoli
Graphics by Marta Lorini

Special thanks to Anna Bloom
Translated by Emily Clement
Interior design by Kay Petronio

10 9 8 7 6 5 4 3 2 1   20 21 22 23 24

Printed in U.S.A.   40

First printing 2020

A SNOWY START

On an **icy** morning in December, I woke up with a start. I had a funny feeling that I was about to go on a **fabumouse** new adventure. My name is Stilton, *Geronimo Stilton*, and I run *The Rodent's Gazette*, the most **famouse** newspaper on Mouse Island!

Brrrr! It was cold enough to **freeze** cheese soup! A breeze **ruffled** my whiskers as I dragged myself out of bed. "I hope it's not going to snow today," I muttered.

I stepped over to the window and sighed. **BIG WHITE** flakes drifted by. "**Frosted feta!** It's already snowing! Who knows what kind of slushy **mess** I'll find today on the streets of New Mouse City!"

All done!
See you later!

I bundled up in my WARMEST winter gear and left the house. Time to head to *The Rodent's Gazette* office and get to WORK!

Despite the weather, the center of town was filled with mice cheerfully making their way to work, or school, or to run errands. No one seemed as bothered by the **SNOW** as me!

I crossed Singing Stone Plaza, the main square in New Mouse City, and looked up in amazement. One of the buildings was covered in an **ENORMOUSE** blue **SHEET**, with a big GOLDEN *R* in the middle of it.

What in the name of cheddar biscuits is that doing there? I wondered.

The building next to that one was also covered up with a sheet! This sheet was **LEOPARD PRINT.**

STRANGE!

Meanwhile, a few passersby SQUEAKED excitedly among themselves, as if they were waiting for something.

I really wanted to stay and see what all the fuss was about, but I was already running late. The news waits for no mouse!

I **stomped** my paws to warm them up and pulled my jacket around me more tightly. Thundering rat tails, I couldn't wait for summer! I shook the **ice** off my whiskers and turned away from the STRANGE, fabric-draped buildings. Maybe later I'd have time to come back and see what was **REALLY** going on here.

MYSTERY MOUSE

I had just reached the office when my cell phone **BUZZED** with a text message!

I didn't recognize the number, and the message was short:

"Geronimo, come to Singing Stone Plaza! Fast as you can! T.S."

Moldy mozzarella!

Moldy mozzarella, how odd. Just then my phone **BUZZED** again, but with an email this time.

I didn't recognize the name, and the message was short:

t.s.@ratt_store.squeak

"Geronimo, come to Singing Stone Plaza! Fast as you can! T.S."

SQUEAKY CHEESE CURDS! The two messages were exactly the same! Just then I saw an elegant *envelope* the color of Fontina cheese sitting on my desk. Printed on the front in GOLD letters  were the words *Ratt Store*, and it had been decorated with a fancy blue seal.

I opened the envelope. Inside was the now very **familiar** message: "Geronimo, come to Singing Stone Plaza! Fast as you can! T.S."

Hmm hmm hmmmm . . . Who was this **mystery mouse**?

As I thought about who this could be, my **whiskers** curling with confusion, I heard a **LOUD** shout coming from the hallway. "Make way, make way, make way!"

Then an even louder shout: "**RATT STORE!**"

I went to see who it was . . .

I had just laid my **paw** on the doorknob when suddenly . . .

The door flew open and hit me right in the **snout**!

I was knocked over and went **rolling** like a wheel of cheese before I could even SQUEAK!

"Heeelllppp!" I cried. Then I fainted!

I came to with a start when someone threw

WATER onto my face, drenching my whiskers and my suit.

"Hey!" I squeaked. "That's **colder** than an icicle!"

When I opened my eyes, a **very** familiar snout stood before me, and a **very** familiar voice squeaked in my ears a few **very** familiar words: "**Cousin! Cousin, Cousin, Cousin! Cousiiiiiiiiin!**"

My head was spinning and I saw stars. The shape standing over me certainly looked like my cousin Trap, but I couldn't

I fell over like a wheel of cheese...

...fainted...

...and came to with a splash of icy water!

be sure. This rodent looked so elegant. He wore a tuxedo, a gold tie, and a top hat.

Slowly, I got up. My vision cleared.

It *was* Trap!

A very fancy Trap!

"Are you the one who came barging through that door?" I asked, rubbing my head with my paw. "You should be more careful. Look at this bump!"

"Bump? What bump? You look marvemouse! But we don't have time for joking around. T.S. needs your help!" a new voice said.

"T.S.? Who is T.S.?" I yelled. "And what kind of help? I am a very busy rodent and I can't just be *dashing* out of the office all the time to help STRANGE mice!"

Just then I noticed that there was someone else behind him.

A female rodent poked her snout through

the door and chuckled. "You're looking at T.S.!" she said.

Confused, I pointed a **paw** at her.

"No, no, silly mouse, it's your cousin. T.S. is the one and only **Trap Stilton!**"

Trap did a twirl and tipped his top hat at me. "Yes, it is I, T.S.! The fabumouse, the marvemouse, the **FANTASTIC** Trap Stilton! And this is **Rita Ratt**, my equally fabumouse new fiancée!"

Rita Ratt, pleasure to meet you!

I am T.S.! Trap Stilton!

THE FABUMOUSE RITA RATT!

I felt like I'd been hit by a brick of cheese. "Fiancée? Trap, since when are you **engaged**?"

Trap just laughed. "Since I met the 𝓁𝓸𝓿𝓮 of my life! I knew right away that she was the **MOUSE OF MY DREAMS...**"

He blew her a **KISS**. "Rita, you're the Brie to my cracker!"

"And you're the Gouda on my cheese plate!" Rita leaned in to plant a smooch on Trap's snout. "SAY CHEESE!" she cried, and the pair snapped a selfie.

Rita squealed. "Light of

Rita Ratt

FIRST NAME: Rita

LAST NAME: Ratt

HER FAMILY: Her grandfather Ronald Ratt accumulated an incredible fortune thanks to his snout for business. He had seven children and many grandchildren, but his favorite is Rita, and he chose her to be his heir!

THE RATT FAMILY PROPERTIES: The Ratts have houses all over the world, a huge yacht, and a luxurious private jet. They drive sports cars and also have a high-tech RV at their disposal. Rita, though, prefers to ride a bicycle. She likes to keep things simple!

HER CAREER: Rita graduated with a degree in communications and is wonderful at organizing events. She loves her job and works with great passion, enthusiasm, and professionalism.

HOW SHE MET TRAP: During one of her events, the launch of a Gorgonzola home fragrance!

HER DREAM: Rita is very romantic and ever since she was young she's dreamed of finding a great love . . . Now she's sure she's found it in Trap!

HER GOAL: To show her family that she can succeed all on her own, Rita is opening a store in New Mouse City: the Ratt Store! It will be a superstore where one can buy "only the best . . . at the best prices!"

Rita Ratt's Family

1. **RONALD RATT:** (Rita's grandfather): Founder of the Ratt family business. A hard worker, he built the Ratt family fortune from the cheese rind up.

2. **ROSA RATT:** (Rita's grandmother): A fearless rodent who built the family fortune alongside her husband.

RONALD AND ROSA'S SEVEN CHILDREN:

3. **REGGIE RATT:** He doesn't work. Instead, he travels the world, enjoying the good life!

4. **ROMEO RATT:** A financial genius, and Rita's father. Rita inherited her intelligence and gift for organization from him.

5. **CHERRY RATT:** Romeo's wife and a famouse architect and interior designer. Rita is their only child.

6 RIGARDA RATT: A world-famous chef.

7 ROCCO RATT: An Mouslympic skiing champion.

8 RAEGAN RATT: Loves fashion and has created a very successful new line of denim clothing.

9 RONDA RATT: Famouse journalist and crime novelist.

10 RANDY RATT: A very snobby rodent; loves sailing and talks only of sailing competitions!

my life, Parmesan on my pasta, cheese to my cracker, show Geronimo the ring you bought me for our engagement!"

Trap blew her a kiss. "Right away, my little cheese curd, my little slice of Swiss, my little dollop of fondue!"

RANCID RICOTTA, this was too much! I put my snout in my paws.

Trap didn't seem to notice me cringing. He leaned over to whisper in my ear; "This ring cost me a lot of cheddar, but it was worth it. Wait until you see how it sparkles! Rita's the most radiant rodent I've ever met — I had to get something that SHINES as much as she does."

He pulled out a silk BOX that was yellow as a slice of American cheese and opened it theatrically, shouting, "Ta-daaa!!"

The inside of the box was blue velvet.

Poking out of it was a massive heart-shaped ruby, set on a gold band. All around the ruby, diamonds shone like little stars.

"Wow," I said. "It . . . um, really sparkles."

Rita stretched out her **PAW** toward the ring and sang out, "Trap's been holding on to the ring so he can get it resized. I can't wait to wear it!"

Trap grinned. "My precious Gouda, my one true mouselet, my deep-fried mozzarella stick — you're my everything!"

Rita bounded over next to me and began to shake my paw vigorously. "I'm so honored to be joining your family! Can I call you Cousin, just like Trap does?

1 "Can I PULL your whiskers just like Trap? 2 Can I sit at your desk just like

Trap? ❸ Can I play **tricks** on you just like Trap? ❹ Can I tell you jokes just like Trap? Can I, can I, can I . . ."

Slimy Swiss cheese! Having Rita around felt like hanging out with two Traps. They did seem to have an awful lot in common . . .

Rita was tall like Trap and bright-eyed like Trap. When she spoke she **hopped** here and there just like Trap. She even giggled like Trap . . . and teased me just like Trap did!

Like Trap, she was also dressed in fancy clothes: She wore an elegant blue silk **dress**

and had a gold purse, gold heels, and expensive *jewelry*. Unlike Trap, though, she had a head of thick blonde hair gathered up in a high bun.

Confused by all her questions, I stuttered over my reply, "J-J-J-Just like Trap? Um, yes, sure, why not, or actually no, not at all . . . even if you do speak like him, you *aren't* Trap!"

"You mean," she squealed, "you don't want me to be a part of the family?" Her snout fell.

Twisting my tail in my paws, I rushed to make her feel better. "Of course you'll be

Blonde hair

Expensive jewelry

Gold purse

Gold high heels

Blue silk dress

part of the **family**, Rita. I'm thrilled that Trap has found such a **fabumouse** rodent to be his partner!" I hesitated. "But I can only take one joker at a time in the family!"

Rita laughed and threw her arms around me happily. "How **marvemouse**! Thank you for making me feel like a Stilton, Geronimo!"

"Um, you're welcome," I said, gently **wiggling** my way out of her embrace.

Just then Trap looked over at the clock and gasped. "Great gobs of stinky cheese, look at the time! We should **shake a tail** and run or we'll be late to the **GRAND OPENING!**"

"Grand opening?" I asked, confused. "What grand opening are you talking about?"

"Of the new **RATT STORE**, of course," Trap cried. He grabbed one of my paws and Rita grabbed the other. "Hurry, Geronimo, we have to cut the ribbon!"

"Everymouse will be waiting on T.S.," Rita said.

Before I could come up with an excuse, I found myself being propelled out of the office and down to the street.

They pushed me into a **LONG** blue car with golden door handles, driven by a uniformed driver, and we took off like a shot.

"Well, I guess I'm coming," I said grumpily. "But before we get there, you have to explain what in New Mouse City Ratt Store is!"

A grin spread across Trap's snout. "The

Ratt Store is the new **SUPERSTORE** opened by the one and only Rita Ratt, selling 'only the best . . . at the best prices!' She'll be offering luxury products at a fraction of the regular price. We'll also have a members-only website, so that select customers can get access to even better deals online."

"'We?'" I repeated.

"Oh yes," Rita cooed. "T.S. here is my store manager and V.I.R. — **Very Important Rodent.**" She reached over to grab Trap's **PAW**.

"We need your support at the grand opening, Geronimo," Trap said. "Rita wants the event to be a big hit!"

Ah. It was all starting to make sense now. Sort of.

I Smell a Ratt . . . Store!

The blue-and-gold car rushed along the streets of New Mouse City to SiNGiNG STONE PLAZA. It SCREECHED to a stop outside the building covered with a BLUE sheet that I had noticed earlier. We hopped out and raced toward the group of rodents assembled outside.

Trap squeezed Rita's paw. "Ready to start the grand opening, my sweet cheddar scone?"

How strange!

"All set, T.S.!" Rita said.

But then she looked around and frowned. "There aren't many **rodents here yet** . . . I thought there would be a **HUGE** crowd!"

A group of workers, all dressed in **blue**-and-gold uniforms, rushed toward her. One of them was wringing his paws together. "Rita, in spite of all the **invitations** we sent, there are only a few mice here. What should we do?"

Rita's eyes *flashed*. She clapped her **PAWS** together and began to shout orders left and right. "Never mind! We'll get started with the group we have! You, turn on the lights! You, hit the music! You, open the doors! And you . . . prepare to greet our guests! Come on! *Let's light a fire under this fondue!*"

All the workers shouted in unison, "Yes, Rita!" They SCURRIED off to do as they'd been told.

But they quickly came scurrying right back. "Rita! EMERGENCY! EMERGENCY!!"

"The lights won't turn on!"

"The stereo won't work!"

"And the front doors won't open!"

Rita's face turned as PALE AS FRESH MOZZARELLA, but she recovered quickly. "Okay, new plan!

① "The lights won't turn on? Light some candles! That will be romantic!

② "If the **stereo** isn't working, turn on the radio! That will be fun!

③ "And if the front doors won't **open**, let everyone in through the garden in the back! That will make us look eco-friendly!"

The lights won't turn on. ①

The stereo isn't working. ②

The front doors won't open. ③

Rita forged ahead with the opening ceremony. She pulled Trap over to a long golden rope attached to the fabric that hid the front of the building. Then she shouted, "Now, the manager of the Ratt Store, Trap 'T.S.' Stilton, will unveil the building!"

Trap **pulled** and **pulled** and **pulled** on the rope with all the strength he had, but the giant sheet wouldn't budge.

I **GROANED**. Everything was going wrong!

Trap grunted and pulled on the rope with all his might. "I . . . think . . . it's . . . stuck," Trap said. Rita lunged forward to help, but it was no use. The blue sheet still covered the building.

The crowd murmured in disappointment, "Awww . . ."

Rita headed toward me. "Geronimo, come help! Follow me!"

Oof!

Rita opened a door at the back of the building and started **CLIMBING** the stairs that led to the roof.

Holey Swiss cheese, it was exhausting!

Up there, we checked the **hooks** that held the sheet up against the front of the building.

HOW STRANGE!

They seemed to be stuck . . . but after pulling on the sheet together, we were finally able to unhook them!

Hurry!

The sheet suddenly fell away, fluttering through the air like an **ENORMOUSE** cheese wrapper. We heard EXCITED shouts from the mice below:

"HOORAY! HOORAY! HOORAY! HOORAY! HOORAY! HOORAY! HOORAY! HOORAY! HOORAY! HOORAY!"

Rita and I **HURRIED** down the steps and back outside. Trap was shouting a welcome into a bullhorn: "Welcome, rodents of New Mouse City! I'm pleased to announce that the Ratt Store is officially open for business! Follow me to the back entrance and we can all go inside!"

I joined in the crowd's applause as we all followed Trap into the *fancy* new store. I turned to congratulate Rita, but she was frowning.

I don't understand!

"I don't understand why the sheet didn't fall . . . and why the lights didn't work. We practiced everything!"

Trap came over and hugged her. "Don't worry, Rita! Everything is fine now. Look!" He pointed a paw at the rodents who were admiring the shiny store interior and heading over to the table of refreshments.

Rita shook her snout. "There can't be any mistakes, T.S.! Everything has to be perfect!" She took a deep breath and walked toward the crowd.

Sweet ricotta ice cream

Gorgonzola tarts

"Welcome inside! Please, try some **faBumouse** treats from our in-store restaurant! We have Gorgonzola tarts served with sweet ricotta ice cream!"

Rita continued talking as she showed the mice where to line up for a tasting. "Everything has been prepared by our four-star chefs, the **DEL TASTY** siblings, Tony and Tina! They're running our new restaurant on the second floor, Twins!, which will prepare a rotating menu of delightful food pairings from all over the world!"

My mouth watered! That sounded *marvemouse*!

IMPOSSIBLE!

The two chefs placed tarts and ice cream on a series of small plates and began handing them out.

"At your service, **RATT STORE** guests! Taste, taste, taste!" they said in unison.

The crowd murmured excitedly.

"Yum, yum, yum!"

TINA AND TONY DEL TASTY

Tina and Tony are twins. They always work as a pair. He specializes in savory dishes, while her specialty is pastry. They come from a family of chefs and learned everything from their famous grandmother Loretta del Tasty. They're excited to have a restaurant in the flashy new Ratt Store, so that they can share their creations with many new rodents!

"All the food looks whisker-licking delicious!"

Rita hovered next to the chefs, twisting her paws together. "Is everything really okay? We've had a lot of problems so far!"

Tony laughed. "Rita, just look at this spread!"

The guests had surrounded the buffet and were gobbling up the Gorgonzola tarts and tasting the sweet ricotta ice cream. Rita looked relieved — but only for a moment.

Suddenly, a large group of mice began coughing and frowning.

"This is disgusting," one rodent said, spitting tart crust back out onto the plate.

Tony and Tina looked as pale as cream cheese toast.

Rita nibbled a tart to see for herself. Her whiskers DROOPED. "This is terrible!

It doesn't taste at all like it did in our run-through." Her eyes **FLASHED**, and the chefs' eyes filled with tears.

Rita banged her plate down on the table. *What is going on?!* "What in the name of **CRISPY CHEESE CURD** is going on here?!"

Quietly, I slid my plate into a nearby potted plant. Too bad! They had looked delicious!

Tony and Tina burst into tears and ran

Oh noooo!

We're ruined!

Gross!

Yuck!

to the kitchen. Rita's expression softened. "Wait!" she called, but they didn't seem to hear.

Trap tugged on Rita's arm. "Forget the snacks, let's just take our guests on a tour!"

Rita managed a smile. "Good idea, T.S." She turned back to the crowd and clapped her paws. "Now for the main event! Let me show you my state-of-the-art superstore! Here you'll find 'only the best . . . at the best prices!' Follow me, please!"

RATT STORE!

ONLY THE BEST . . . AT THE BEST PRICES!

CLOTHING, ACCESSORIES, SPORTS
EQUIPMENT, JEWELRY, PERFUME,
FURNITURE, HOME GOODS . . .

EVERYTHING YOU NEED AT FABUMOUSE PRICES!

WHAT'S MORE, ALL OUR PRODUCTS
CAN ALSO BE BOUGHT ONLINE!

RATT STORE, GROUND FLOOR

1. ENTRANCE
2. ESCALATORS
3. RESTROOMS
4. TOYS
5. BEAUTY
6. JEWELRY AND FASHION ACCESSORIES
7. SPECIAL OCCASION CLOTHING
8. CLOTHING
9. BOOKS, STATIONERY, AND MUSIC
10. SPORTS EQUIPMENT AND TRAVEL
11. HOME GOODS

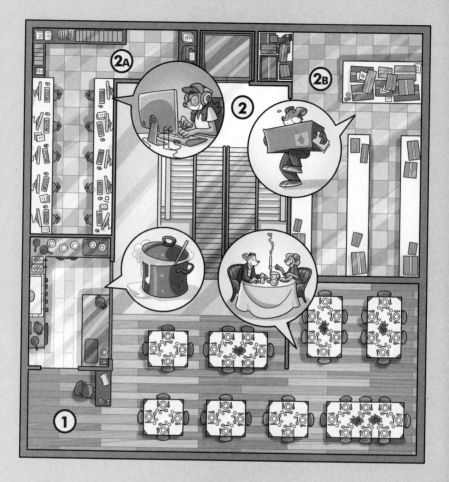

RATT STORE, SECOND FLOOR

1. TWINS! RESTAURANT
2. ONLINE SALES DEPARTMENT
2A. ONLINE ORDER PICKUP DESK
2B. WAREHOUSE (HERE THE ITEMS ORDERED ONLINE ARE PACKED UP AND SENT ALL OVER MOUSE ISLAND.)

Trap welcomed all the mouselets into the home goods department. He ran his paw down a row of curtains. "Look, ladies and gentlemice, feel how soft this silk is . . ."

Trap examined the curtain in his paw more closely and gasped. "Rita," he whispered. "Sweet moldy cheese rind, these curtains are filled with holes!"

HOLEY CURTAINS!

Rita's eyes narrowed. "That's IMPOSSIBLE!" she cried. "Quick, take everyone to a different part of the store! Geronimo, help me take these curtains down!"

I hurried to help her as Trap led the group into the furniture area. "Now, ladies and gentlemice, look how **SOLID** this furniture is . . ."

But just then Rita and I heard a

BROKEN FURNITURE!

CRASH. We dropped the curtains we had been holding and *raced* over to the furniture department.

We found Trap holding his paw and squealing. "The dresser collapsed on me!" he cried. "Melty mozzarella sticks, this furniture is all ROTTED AWAY!"

Impossible!

Rita's whiskers quivered. "IMPOSSIBLE!"

I peered down at the CRUMPLED pile of wood. How could a brand-new piece of furniture just fall apart? Trap wasn't *that* strong . . .

Rita quickly steered all the rodents away from the mess. "Now Trap will take you to the dishware department!" She reached into the POCKET of her dress and pulled out a small mouse-to-mouse radio. "Cleanup in furniture!" she squeaked into it.

The radio CRACKLED. "On it like pimento cheese on crackers, Rita," said a worker.

Just then we heard another call from Trap: "Rita, come look!"

"What now!" she muttered as we *hurried* over to see what the problem was.

"All these plates are **cracked**," Trap said, holding one up.

"IMPOSSIBLE!" Rita screeched.

I was beginning to think Rita didn't know what the word IMPOSSIBLE meant. Suddenly, a strange **smell** wafted under my nose. It was worse than RANCID RICOTTA!

"Something **stinks**!" one of the rodents in the crowd said, waving his paw under his nose as we passed by the store's restrooms.

"Look out, Rita!" Trap SCREAMED.

I looked over to see a wave of **stinky water** rushing under the bathroom doors and across the floor — heading right for us!

Heeelp!

Let's get out of here!

Hurry!

Everything is going wrong!

Squeak!!! Every rodent for themselves!

All the guests made a run for the exits, including

Rip!

The train of her dress tore!

me! I wanted to help Trap and Rita, but not if it meant getting soaked in dirty water!

I followed the other mice to the escalators, hoping to escape the dirty water by going upstairs, but they were out of order. **OF COURSE!** So all the rodents began to scramble back toward the exit.

Rita and Trap followed close behind me. "Now the escalators are **BROKEN**," Rita squeaked. "Absolutely everything has gone wrong!"

Snap!

One of her heels broke!

Her mascara started to run!

Trap patted her arm, but Rita was too upset to notice. As we reached the steps at the back entrance, she stumbled a bit. Then the train of her **dress** tore with a sharp **RIP**! And then one of her **heels** suddenly broke: **SNAP**!

Her false eyelashes came off, leaving a **LONG** trail of black **mascara** on her face: *swish*!

SQUEAK!

Rita let out a loud **squeak**. "I planned this store opening **PERFECTLY**! I don't understand how so many things could have gone so very wrong!"

LONG LOST FRIENDS

Rita sat down in a heap on the stairs leading to the superstore's back entrance. She let out a **SOB** and Trap passed her one of his handkerchiefs. All the mice who had gathered for the grand opening hustled out the door in a hurry. I had a feeling there wouldn't be repeat customers anytime soon. Even the store employees were leaving to avoid the smelly bathroom flood.

Soon, only the three of us were left.

Trap tried to make Rita feel better. "Don't be a worryrat, my marvemouse mozzarella. This was just one day — and a small group of mice. We'll get everything fixed and sell all our stuff like CHEDDAR HOTCAKES before you know it."

But Rita kept sniffling. "T.S., we needed to make a *good impression* . . . and I worked so hard to plan everything . . . How could this have happened?"

Then she blew her nose in Trap's *handkerchief*. "What will my family say? The family name means so much to them!"

I picked up the torn piece of Rita's dress to hand

Marvemouse mozzarella!

Sob Sob Sob!

back to her and noticed something VERY STRANGE. The edge of the dress didn't look torn at all. Instead, there was a crisp cut line. Some **RASCALLY** rodent had cut the dress and sewed it loosely back together!

That's why it had torn off so easily! I searched around the stairs until I found the heel of Rita's shoe. Just as I suspected, this also looked like it had been tampered with. It looked like someone had broken the heel and then **glued** it back to the shoe with some kind of **sticky** putty.

Toasted cheese! Who would want to ruin Rita and her grand opening?

I waved Trap over and whispered my suspicions. His ears **trembled**.

"We must get to the bottom of this!" he hissed.

"I agree," I said. "I'll text *Hercule Poirat*, the best investigator in New Mouse City!"

"That's a great idea, Cousin!" Trap agreed.

But Poirat didn't text me back himself. Instead, I got an automated message, along with a picture of Poirat in some kind of **tropical** place. The message read: "Hello from paradise, my friend! I am on vacation in the Happy Islands, sprawled out on the beach, drinking cheddar punch

He's on vacation!

in the shade of PALM trees! I will try and reply to you when I am back!"

While I tried to think of some other idea for how to help Rita, my cell phone rang.

RRRRING, RRRRING, RRRRRING!

I saw a number I recognized right away: It belonged to CREEPELLA VON CACKLEFUR!

"Hi, Creepella," I answered. "I can't really talk right now. I'm helping a friend at the new superstore in Singing Stone Plaza."

"Geronimo! You've been such a help. I'm forever grateful," Rita squeaked behind me.

Through the phone, I could hear Creepella make a sniffing noise. "Oh, I see," she said coldly. "Well, if your new *friend* is in need of so much help, I'll come over myself to lend a PAW. Singing Stone Plaza, you say?"

"No need, Creepella! Talk to you later!" I ended the call and **groaned**.

Trap and Rita went inside the store to assess the damage, and I followed them up the stairs and into the sports equipment department.

Trap and Rita began examining all the items on display and making note of what seemed broken or missing.

I was taking a quick rest behind some mannequins,

How dare you!

when I heard my name bellowed from across the room:

"Geronimo Stilton!"

CREEPELLA! She looked a *little* upset that I had hung up on her.

Her eyes sparkled under the store lights.

"Furry feta pancakes, I can't believe you would hang up on me like that!" she said, putting her paws on her hips.

"Creepella, I-I-I-I," I stammered, but was saved by the appearance of Rita, who had just come out of a supply closet, carrying a broom.

"I'm sorry, miss, we're currently closed for some, um, tweaks before opening. But we'd love to have you come back when —"

Rita stopped abruptly as Creepella turned around.

Creepella **yelped** loudly and tossed her paws in the air. "Darling!"

I blinked in SURPRISE. Trap came around the corner as Creepella and Rita shared an enthusiastic **HUG**.

"Small world, Cousin," Trap said.

Rita and Creepella clasped paws. "How are you?" Rita asked.

"I'm **fabumouse**," Creepella said. "It's so good to see you!"

"How do you two know each other?" Trap asked.

They laughed. "We were classmates in school, and we've been great friends ever since," Creepella said.

Rita gestured to Trap. "Do you know T.S., my new fiancé?"

Creepella **giggled**. "Of course I know him! He's Geronimo's cousin! But I didn't know you were opening this **marvemouse** new store!" Creepella gestured around her.

Rita sighed. "I sent you an invitation! It must have gotten lost. A lot of things have been going wrong . . ." Rita trailed off and her whiskers **drooped**.

Creepella **hugged** her again. "Come on, Rita, tell me everything. I'm here to help.

THAT'S WHAT FRIENDS ARE FOR!"

We all sat down on some chairs Trap had pulled over from the furniture department, and Rita went through what had happened during the failed grand opening.

Creepella listened carefully, her expression **darkening** with each new BAD thing that had happened.

"I just didn't expect to have such bad luck on the biggest day of my life," Rita finished. She sighed loudly and Trap patted her paw.

Creepella turned to me and we shared a quiet glance. I could tell she thought the same thing I did. This wasn't just BAD LUCK. This was **sabotage**.

SOMETHING STINKS!

Creepella thought for a moment, tapping the side of her chair. "Rita, something about this whole situation SMELLS worse than Gorgonzola left out in the SUN."

Rita twisted her paws in her lap NERVOUSLY. "You think someone ruined my opening on purpose, don't you?"

We all nodded.

"But who would want to do that?" she asked, looking shocked.

"We'll find out who's behind it — right, Geronimo?" Trap said.

Squeak! "Well, that seems more like a job for a professional —" I started to say, but Creepella cut me off.

"Of course we're going to help! Step one

is to FIX everything that was **broken** — starting with those bathrooms!" She wrinkled her snout and took out her phone. Creepella has all the best plumbers,

Of course we'll help!

electricians, and repairmice on *speed* dial.

"Quick, come to the Ratt Store! I need you, as *quickly* as your paws can bring you. It will be worth it — trust me!"

Holey Swiss cheese, Creepella worked fast!

"Come on, Geronimo," Creepella said. "Let's take a look around and see what we can find out."

I scurried after her, and we searched the superstore, cataloging everything that had been *sabotaged*.

CREEPELLA'S INVESTIGATION!

1. STOLEN INVITATIONS. I discovered that almost all the invitations for the grand opening were hidden in the Ratt Store storage room. That's why there were so few rodents at the grand opening!

2. RIGGED POWER LINES. My electrician found that the central power lines were cut! That's why the lights and music didn't work, and why the main doors wouldn't open.

3. BROKEN HOOKS. The sheet covering the building was supposed to fall gracefully, but the hooks holding it had been tampered with.

4. DISGUSTING FOOD. The sugar container had been replaced with salt, which is why the tarts were so terrible!

5. HOLEY CURTAINS. A hole punch was used on the fabric, to mimic moth holes!

6. BROKEN FURNITURE. Holes were drilled in the furniture, to make it seem rotten.

7. CRACKED PLATES. Someone ruined the dishware!

8. WAVE OF STINKY WATER. My plumber found that the toilets had been intentionally clogged with whole rolls of toilet paper!

9. RITA'S DRESS. My personal tailor confirmed that the train of her dress had been cut off and resewn with weak stitches.

 10. RITA'S HIGH HEEL. My cobbler proved that the heel had been broken and recently glued back on.

After our very thorough search, Creepella presented all our findings to Rita.

"Do you have any idea who could be out to get you?" I asked. "Are there any mice who might have a grudge against you or your family?"

Rita shrugged. "I don't think so."

Just then we heard the sound of voices, as if many **mice** had just arrived. We peered out of the superstore and saw that right in

Here we are.

It'll start soon!

front of the Ratt Store a huge crowd had gathered.

We went outside and I approached one of the rodents. "What's happening?" I asked.

"It's the grand opening of the No Store, of course! It's a luxury superstore that also has an elite online membership for special deals and discounts. I bought designer sneakers, a wedding dress, and a

shower curtain this morning, all on the same website, with just a squeak of a button. When the No Store opens, I can go in and pick them up."

Behind me, Rita squealed. "But that's exactly the idea behind the Ratt Store!"

The mouse we had been talking to pointed to the building next to us, covered in a leopard-print sheet. "Look, they're about to open it up . . ."

Just then a LONG luxury limousine with dark windows and a leopard-print paint job pulled up. One of the windows went down slowly BZZZZZ! Out popped a snout I knew all too well. A voice I knew all too well hissed in our direction: "Why hello, Stilton! How not nice to see you."

It was none other than . . . Madame No!

JUST SAY NO!

Rita's face went as pale as a bowl of creamy cheese soup. "That's Madame No, my family's great nemesis!"

Creepella was shocked. "Madame No and your family are ENEMiES? I didn't know that!"

Rita sighed. "I had mostly forgotten about it, but Madame No's mother knew my grandfather Ronald. They used to be really good friends. Then something went wrong. I don't know the details, but I think it involved a cheese wheel company they had both invested in. Since then, her family's done everything they can to ruin my grandfather . . . But we haven't heard from her in years . . ."

Rita stopped speaking as Madame No got

out of the car, adjusted her dark sunglasses, and turned to us. "Oh, look who we have here, little Rita Ratt . . . granddaughter of Ronald Ratt. FABUMOUSE store you have here. It's a pity your grand opening wasn't such a success . . ."

"The opening just had a few HICCUPS, that's all!" Creepella interrupted angrily.

"Yeah!" Trap said. "The Ratt Store is going to be the biggest thing since sliced cheese!"

Madame No peered over her sunglasses. Her eyes narrowed. "Well, I guess we'll see about that, won't we?" She pulled her leopard-print coat more snugly around her shoulders. "If that's your goal, you might want to do something about

Nice broom!

those overflowed toilets. Nice broom, by the way." She grinned. "Tell your grandfather I said *hello*," she said, and walked away.

Madame No took a step toward the enormouse, leopard print–covered building. "Welcome! Thanks so much for coming to New Mouse City's best luxury goods superstore!"

The crowd cheered.

Madame No turned to **LOOK** directly at us as she gave the rope attached to the sheet a MiGHTY pull. Unlike the Ratt Store's covering, this one slipped right off and dropped to the ground. The TALL building had a grand, gold-plated sign that read:

Madame No clapped her paws. "Hit the **LIGHTS**! Turn on the **MUSIC**! Open the **doors**! Serve the **SNACKS**! Give the crowd a **TOUR** of every department!"

Worker mice in crisp new uniforms suddenly came out from everywhere, leading guests inside and handing out food.

It looked like a well-choreographed DANCE.

And suddenly, it was! A swarm of workers in leopard-print outfits marched to the front of the building. A spotlight *beamed* and music with a thumping beat started. The talented mice began an elaborate dance routine.

"Holey Swiss cheese," I muttered as one of the dancing mouselets lifted Madame No high in the air and twirled her around.

The audience CLAPPED their paws to the beat. I even caught Trap swaying to the music!

As Madame No swept past us, carried by one of the dancers, she leaned down. "This is how you open a store, dear," she called. As the music ended, and Madame No returned to the front of the building, the crowd erupted in a frenzy of cheers and applause.

HOORAY! HOORAY! HOORAY! HOORAY! HOORAY! HOORAY! HOORAY! HOORAY! HOORAY! HOORAY! HOORAY!

"I've never seen anything like that," Creepella said, shaking her snout.

"Me neither," I agreed.

Rita didn't say anything, but her shoulders slumped.

Trap looked around at our sad snouts and groaned. "Don't be such worryrats! She may have a **dance routine**, and a flashy sign, and very delicious-looking CHEESE STRAWS, but she doesn't have Rita!"

Rita smiled slightly. "That's very kind, T.S., but I just don't know how I'm going to compete with all of that." She pointed a paw at the long line of excited-looking mice waiting to get into the No Store.

Squeak! I didn't know how she was going to compete with that, either!

A STILTON FAMILY PROMISE

Back inside the Ratt Store, Creepella and I settled onto some couches in the furniture department. Creepella took out the NOTES she'd made on all the damage and scrolled through photos on her phone.

"There must be some clue here as to who did all this," she said. "Did you hear what Madame No said out there?"

"She said a lot of things," I muttered.

Creepella ROLLED her eyes. "I meant one specific thing. She told Rita that she should do something about 'those OVERFLOWED toilets.' How would she know about that —"

"Unless she'd done it herself!" I finished.

"Or hired someone to do it," Creepella said. "Quick, let's go find Rita!"

Rita was SHOCKED when we told her our theory. "I can't believe that she would stoop that low. Madame No has held a **grudge** against our family for a long time, but what she did to the store seems excessive, even for her."

Trap **HUGGED** Rita. "Don't be a worryrat, my adorable cheddar muffin. The *Stilton family* will help you! And when we make a promise, we always keep it! Right, Cousin?"

I put my paw over my heart. "Oh yes, Rita, the Stilton family will help you!"

Creepella clasped

her paws. "Dear Rita, we'll figure out what to do about Madame No's **sabotage**. My workers are fixing everything as we squeak."

"And we'll expose Madame No!" I added. "Not only did she **ruin** your grand opening, she's stolen the very idea for the superstore!"

Trap **frowned**. "Well, Rita, I guess the **silver rind** on this stinky cheese is that you must have come up with a pretty **marvemouse** idea for Madame No to be so threatened by it."

Rita sighed. "I guess so. All I wanted to do was open a store that would revolutionize the shopping experience, bring happiness to New Mouse City rodents, and make my family proud! Was that too much to ask?"

SQUEAK!

To break the **GLOOMY** mood, Creepella laughed loudly. "One day, when I get married,

I will register for all of my presents here at the Ratt Store!"

Rita squealed. "Why that would be **fabumouse**! I was planning to have a whole wedding gift program, with a special mouselet to show you around and help select the BEST of the BEST items!" Her eyes sparkled. "Perhaps you could test the service!"

My whiskers trembled. "We would love that!" Creepella cried.

We'll help you!

Oh, Geronimo!

Rita smiled for the first time in hours. "Marvemouse! I can get a photographer to take pictures of you going through the process, and use them to advertise the store! Oooh, I can't wait!"

Just then we could hear someone pounding on the front doors of the Ratt Store.

"I'll go see who it is!" I yelped, and raced over to check. Saved by the knock!

THE RATT DIAMOND!

At the front doors were Benjamin and Trappy, along with their **friend** Bugsy Wugsy! I opened the door for them and led them back to the group.

"Trap texted that you all needed some **HELP**. So here we are!" Benjamin said.

We explained the situation.

"That Madame No is always up to no good," Trappy said grimly.

Benjamin rubbed his WHiSKeRS thoughtfully. "How are we going to prove that Madame No

We're here to help!

sabotaged the grand opening of the Ratt Store?"

Creepella's eyes *flashed* and a crafty grin spread across her snout. "I think I might have an idea . . . When you need to catch a rat, you have to set a trap!" She brought her paws together in a dramatic clap, making me JUMP.

"What kind of **trap**?" Bugsy Wugsy asked.

"We'll lure her here with something she'll surely try to steal . . . and then we'll catch her with her paws in the cheese drawer! Rita, call your family and ask them to send you the Ratt Diamond. We'll say it's to help celebrate the new grand opening."

Then she turned to my cousin. "Trap, you prepare an armored CRYSTAL display case and lock it with a key. We'll use that to hold the Ratt Diamond when it arrives."

Then she looked at me. "Geronimo, you call *The Rodent's Gazette*. Spread the news that Monday morning the Ratt Store will have a new **grand opening**, during which they will display to the public, for the very first time, the famouse Ratt Diamond, also known as the **Great Egg**! Madame No will be unable to resist trying to **STEAL** it."

Finally, Creepella turned to Benjamin, Trappy, and Bugsy Wugsy. "And you, mice . . .

THE RATT DIAMOND

A beautiful famous diamond Ronald Ratt bought for his wife, Rosa. It's known as the Great Egg because it's the size of a chicken egg. It shines with pure light and reflects the seven colors of the rainbow. It's a priceless gem, which is why it hasn't been exhibited in years and stays locked in the family vault.

roll up your sleeves, because we're going to help organize and clean up this superstore from top to bottom! After that, I've got a special job for you to do . . ."

"You got it, Creepella!" they cried together.

Everyone scurried off to do their part. Finally! A chance to beat Madame No at her own game!

We worked the whole weekend, until the **STORE** was all clean and shining again. Sunday evening, the night before the grand

opening, the Ratt Diamond arrived in an armored van.

Rita placed the diamond in its special CRYSTAL case herself. Then we all stood back to admire it. It sparkled in the glow of the overhead lights, almost seeming to shine from within.

"Holey Swiss cheese!" I said. "That's one impressive diamond. Madame No will definitely want that on her trophy shelf."

"I hope so," Creepella said. "But don't be a worryrat, Rita, we won't let her take it!" Creepella looked as determined as I'd ever seen her. Watch out, Madame No!

"What do we do now?" Trap asked.

"Now we wait," Creepella said.

"Are you sure that Madame No will try to steal the Ratt Diamond?" Benjamin asked.

Rita sighed sadly. "I'm sure of it. She won't pass up a chance this big to embarrass me — and take home such a treasure."

"We'll catch her **cheese-handed**, Rita! I can feel it in my WHiSKeRS!" Creepella said.

Night fell, and we hid ourselves on the second floor, where the diamond was displayed.

We squeezed ourselves behind the bar in the restaurant. From there, we had a good view of the lighted case.

Trap patted me on the back so hard I almost tipped over. "You should do the first patrol, Cousin!" He gestured out to the inky darkness of the deserted floor.

Gulp!

Fried feta, I didn't want to go out there alone! But I took a deep breath and stepped out from behind the bar. Slowly, I went from floor to floor, looking for any signs of trouble. In the darkness, I stumbled over a lot of things — but none of them

You go first!

Squeak!

NIGHTTIME PATROL INSIDE

1 I TRIPPED ON A RUG IN THE PERFUME DEPARTMENT.

2 I RAN INTO A MANNEQUIN IN THE WOMEN'S CLOTHING DEPARTMENT.

3 A PAIR OF SKIS FELL ON MY HEAD IN THE SPORTS EQUIPMENT DEPARTMENT.

4 I STEPPED IN AN OPEN POT OF GLUE IN THE STATIONERY DEPARTMENT.

THE RATT STORE

I TRIPPED ON A TRAIN IN THE TOY DEPARTMENT.

5

I BUMPED INTO A BOX OF SHIRTS IN THE MEN'S CLOTHING DEPARTMENT.

7

BY THE TIME I MADE IT BACK TO THE SECOND FLOOR, I WAS A WRECK!

were Madame No! Finally, I returned to the second floor, my heart **thumping** wildly in my chest.

"Well?" Creepella whispered.

"Quiet as a mouse for now!" I whispered back.

We waited for hours, taking turns doing sweeps of the building. Finally, we heard the floor squeak and saw a beam of light break through the darkness.

Great gobs of moldy mozzarella,

It's the thief.

someone was in here with us!

"Get ready," Rita whispered. "It's the **thief**."

Surprise, Thief!

Creepella leaped forward and grabbed the figure by the tail. "Surprise, thief! I've got you! There will be no escape now!"

The thief fell forward and let out a high-pitched **SQUEAK**. Creepella was still holding on to her tail, so she pitched forward as well.

As they fell, they *smacked* into a shelf of crystal glasses, which crashed to the ground and broke into a thousand pieces.

Benjamin raced over to turn on the lights.

Lying on the ground, amid the **rubble**, was a mysterious blonde mouse wearing a black catsuit and a black mask. In the fall, she had dropped a **leopard-print** backpack and a **leopard-print** flashlight.

Rita stepped forward to remove the MASK. We all gasped.

It was the SHADOW, the most FAMOUSE thief in New Mouse City! She was known for doing Madame No's bidding.

"What a lovely leopard-print backpack you have there," Rita said. "It looks like the perfect size to conceal the Ratt Diamond!"

I've got you!

Squeak!

The Shadow stayed silent and refused to look at any of us.

"Madame No sure will be disappointed this time!" Trap gloated.

"How dare you!" boomed a familiar voice from across the second floor.

It was Madame No herself!

"How dare you accuse us of attempting to steal your little diamond!" she continued. "All you have is evidence that we broke in to

check up on the competition. We haven't taken a thing." Madame No Smiled smugly.

Creepella also smiled. "We have a little more than that. Benjamin — play the video!"

What in the wobbly whiskers are they talking about? I wondered. A screen came down from the ceiling and a video of Madame No in her superstore started playing.

"It was a top secret mission," Benjamin whispered to me. "Madame No secured her building against all kinds of high-tech threats, but she didn't count on a couple of young rodents with cell phones."

A smile crept across my snout as the video played. On-screen, Madame No CACKLED with the Shadow. "No one will ever know I stole Rita Ratt's idea for a luxury superstore — and now I'll have her precious family **diamond**, too!"

In front of us, Madame No turned as pale as a bowl of Swiss cheese SOUP. After a moment of silence, she dropped to her knees. "Please, you can't show this video to anyone. It would **ruin** me!"

"Like you tried to **ruin** me?" Rita asked **COLDLY**.

Madame No didn't have a response to that. "Look," she said finally. "Our families have been **feuding** for a while. Your grandfather has sabotaged businesses of mine in the past, too!" Rita looked skeptical, but Madame No continued. "I'm sure we can come to some sort of agreement. I'll pay for all the damage and I'll close the No Store!"

Now Rita looked less **angry**.

GRANDFATHER RONALD
GRANDMOTHER ROSA

"That's a pretty good offer . . . but I'll have to ask my grandfather. He supported the Ratt Store and he'll want to know you tried to destroy it."

Madame No's WHISKERS drooped as Rita made the call.

While Rita was dialing, I noticed that the Shadow was tiptoeing off into the darkness. I ran after her, but lost her after she ducked into a darkened stairwell.

As I jogged back, I heard Rita talking to her grandfather. She told him everything that had happened over the last few days, ending with Madame No's offer.

Rita listened for a LOOONG time, nodding and murmuring as we all anxiously waited to see what he had said. Finally, the call ended. "Sounds good, Grandfather. I'll let you know how it goes!"

We accept your offer!

Hooray!

Rita gives her the good news . . .

But you must work for it!

. . . and the bad news!

She hung up and turned to Madame No. "I have **good** news and BAD news. Which do you want to hear first?"

"The good news first!" Madame No squeaked.

Rita smiled. "The **good news** is that the Ratt family accepts your offer. We won't show the video to anyone."

"I really appreciate that!" Madame No said.

Rita held up a paw. "But now for the BAD news: In addition to the other terms, you must also provide one month's free labor here at the Ratt Store."

Madame No's whiskers trembled. "Um, manual labor is not really where I shine," she mummbled, looking for a way out of it.

"Very well. When do I begin?" she said, sighing.

Trap stepped forward and clapped her on the shoulder. "Right now!"

He handed her a Ratt Store uniform, a BROOM, and a dustpan. "The Shadow knocked over some glasses when she was trying to steal my fiancée's precious family heirloom. You can start by sweeping all of that up!"

Madame No trudged over to the pile of broken glass and grumpily began to sweep.

Rita pointed to a SIGN on the wall that read:

HERE WE SMILE,
THROUGH WORK AND PLAY,
FOR THE TIME TO BE
HAPPY IS . . . TODAY!

"Madame No," she called. "Here at the Ratt Store, we always smile . . . through all we do. What's good for all is good for you!"

"Very well," Madame No muttered. She showed her teeth in what passed for a Madame No smile and went back to work.

I yawned. Time to be heading home! "Good night, everyone!" I called. "Or, I guess good morning!" I waved a paw at the group and headed for the exit. I couldn't believe how easily we'd trapped Madame No. At least I wouldn't be seeing her for a while . . .

WHAT A SUPER STORE!

A few weeks later, I was working at *The Rodent's Gazette* when Thea barged into my office. "Geronimo! I could tell from the street what terrible condition your curtains are in! They have more holes than a slice of Swiss cheese."

I shrugged.

They're in bad shape!

I guess?

"You're an important news mouse! You need to make a better first impression."

"Well, these are antiques," I said. "They were originally Grandfather William's."

Thea touched them. "Hmm, they may be antiques, but they're faded and FALLING APART!"

I looked closer. "I guess you're right . . ."

"Of course I'm right! Come on, let's go visit Rita and Trap at the **RATT STORE**! I bet they'll have just the thing for you. We could just order them online, but I want to take a walk. Geronimo, let's go!"

Thea took my arm and steered me out of the office.

Before long, we had arrived at the Ratt Store's impressive building. When we went inside, we were immediately met by **Rita** and **Trap**.

"Hi, friends," Rita said. "What can we help you with?"

I looked around. "I need some new YELLOW CURTAINS for my office," I said. "Thea thinks the ones I have now aren't **good** enough." I rolled my eyes.

Thea gave me a playful pat on the arm. "They aren't! They look like two old pieces of cheddar flapping in the breeze!"

Rita grinned. "I'm sure we can find you

something **fabumouse**, Geronimo! And they will be on the house!"

"I couldn't possibly accept them as a **gift**," I protested.

"Of course you can! Without you and Creepella, I wouldn't still have the Ratt Store! I **insist**."

I **hugged** Rita. "Thank you, Rita," I said. "Every time I look at them, I will think of our **mouserific** friendship!"

How marvemouse to see you!

Then Rita turned to Trap. "T.S., what kind of curtains do you think are best for Cousin Geronimo? Stripes? Polka dots? Something with ꭆuffⅼes, perhaps? Or *fringe*?"

Trap looked thoughtfully at me. **Squeak!** All the options sounded a little too flashy!

"If I know Geronimo — and I do! — then I'm going to say he'd ⅼove those new **velvet** curtains the color of lightly toasted cheese we just got in."

I sighed with relief. "Those sound perfect!"

"Let's head to home goods!" Rita said, waving us forward. "You can meet our newest sales associate." She WINKED at Trap.

We headed to the home goods area, and who should be sitting behind the sales desk? Madame No!

"Hello! I forgot that you'd still be working here!" I said. "I'm looking for **velvet** curtains, the color of toasted cheese."

Madame No gritted her teeth. "Fontina face," she muttered under her breath, typing something into her computer.

"What was that, Madame No?" Rita asked. She smiled sweetly and pointed a paw up at the customer service sign on the wall that read:

HERE WE SMILE,
THROUGH WORK AND PLAY,
FOR THE TIME TO BE
HAPPY IS . . . TODAY!

Madame No forced a slight smile onto her face. "So, Mr. Stilton, curtains you said? Ah yes, I see that we have lots of velvet curtains in stock. Come with me, and I'll show you the options."

I followed her over to the display racks, and she helped me choose a new set of curtains. They were the perfect color!

Madame No carefully folded up the curtains I'd selected and put them in a bag for me. "Here you go. Thanks for choosing the **RATT STORE**."

I took the bag and started to walk away. But then I turned back. "Madame No?" I called.

"Yes?" she said. "Did you need anything else?"

"No," I said. "I just wanted to let you know that I can see that you're not all bad . . . if you ever want to make PEACE . . . maybe even be friends, I'd like that."

Madame No stared at me in silence.

I put out my paw to shake hers, and she took it, with a small smile and a nod. Then she frowned again and stalked away.

We could be friends!

Thea and I walked back together, while the moon was just starting to appear in the crisp winter sky.

"Who knew Madame No would actually be kind of good at working in a **superstore**?" I said.

"There's more to her than **EVIL** plotting and a desire for **world domination**, I guess!" Thea laughed.

"I guess so!" I said. "Even **stinky cheese** sometimes tastes **delicious**!"

Thea and I rounded the corner toward *The Rodent's Gazette* office. Thea sped up her pace. "Hurry, Geronimo! I want to see how your new curtains look!"

I jogged after Thea. I was **one lucky mouse** to have a sister like her!

What an **ADVENTURE** it was to help save the Ratt Store. Maybe after this

experience, Madame No will change her troublemaking ways. Maybe we could all even become FRieNds?

SQUEAK! Probably not!! But it's okay. The Ratt superstore is super popular, and I have plenty of friends. For now, I'll just enjoy the peace and quiet while Madame No is kept busy working for Rita!

Until the next adventure, a fabumouse hug from your rodent friend,

Geronimo Stilton!

Don't miss a single fabumouse adventure!

Up Next:

Don't miss the graphic novel by Geronimo and Tom Angleberger, artist and longtime fan!

The Sewer Rat Stink

A stinky smell is taking over New Mouse City! No mouse can live like this! Geronimo and his best friend Hercule, the private detective, head underground into the sewer world of Mouse Island to investigate. Can they save the city from the stench?

Visit Geronimo in every universe!

Spacemice

Geronimo Stiltonix and his crew are out of this world!

Cavemice

Geronimo Stiltonoot, an ancient ancestor, is friends with the dinosaurs in the Stone Age!

Micekings

Geronimo Stiltonord lives amongst the dragons in the ancient far north!

Don't miss any of these exciting Thea Sisters adventures!

Thea Stilton and the
Dragon's Code

Thea Stilton and the
Mountain of Fire

Thea Stilton and the
Ghost of the Shipwreck

Thea Stilton and the
Secret City

Thea Stilton and the
Mystery in Paris

Thea Stilton and the
Cherry Blossom Adventure

Thea Stilton and the
Star Castaways

Thea Stilton: Big Trouble
in the Big Apple

Thea Stilton and the
Ice Treasure

Thea Stilton and the
Secret of the Old Castle

Thea Stilton and the
Blue Scarab Hunt

Thea Stilton and the
Prince's Emerald

Thea Stilton and the
Mystery on the Orient Express

Thea Stilton and the
Dancing Shadows

Thea Stilton and the
Legend of the Fire Flowers

Thea Stilton and the
Spanish Dance Mission

**Thea Stilton and the
Journey to the Lion's Den**

**Thea Stilton and the
Great Tulip Heist**

**Thea Stilton and the
Chocolate Sabotage**

**Thea Stilton and the
Missing Myth**

**Thea Stilton and the
Lost Letters**

**Thea Stilton and the
Tropical Treasure**

**Thea Stilton and the
Hollywood Hoax**

**Thea Stilton and the
Madagascar Madness**

**Thea Stilton and the
Frozen Fiasco**

**Thea Stilton and the
Venice Masquerade**

**Thea Stilton and the
Niagara Splash**

**Thea Stilton and the
Riddle of the Ruins**

**Thea Stilton and the
Phantom of the Orchestra**

**Thea Stilton and the
Black Forest Burglary**

**Thea Stilton and the
Race for the Gold**

**Thea Stilton and the
Rainforest Rescue**

Don't miss any of my fabumouse special editions!

THE JOURNEY TO ATLANTIS

THE SECRET OF THE FAIRIES

THE SECRET OF THE SNOW

THE CLOUD CASTLE

THE TREASURE OF THE SEA

THE LAND OF FLOWERS

THE SECRET OF THE CRYSTAL FAIRIES

THE DANCE OF THE STAR FAIRIES

THE MAGIC OF THE MIRROR

Thea Stilton

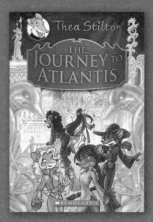

Secret Fairies

Don't miss any of these exciting series featuring the Thea Sisters!

Treasure Seekers

Mouseford Academy

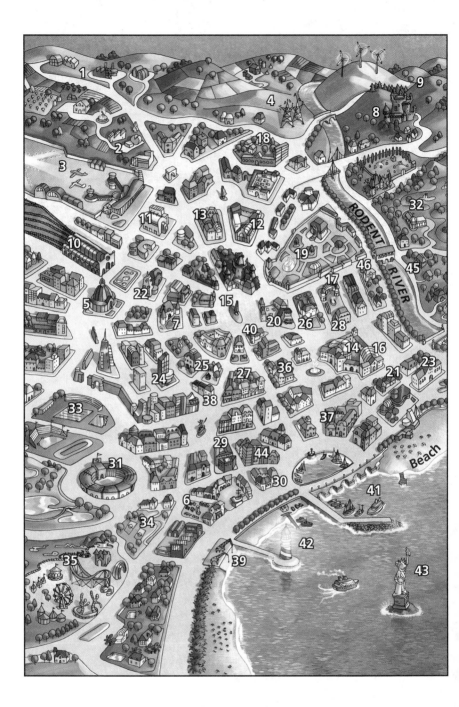

Map of New Mouse City

Map of Mouse Island

1. Big Ice Lake
2. Frozen Fur Peak
3. Slipperyslopes Glacier
4. Coldcreeps Peak
5. Ratzikistan
6. Transratania
7. Mount Vamp
8. Roastedrat Volcano
9. Brimstone Lake
10. Poopedcat Pass
11. Stinko Peak
12. Dark Forest
13. Vain Vampires Valley
14. Goose Bumps Gorge
15. The Shadow Line Pass
16. Penny Pincher Castle
17. Nature Reserve Park
18. Las Ratayas Marinas
19. Fossil Forest
20. Lake Lake
21. Lake Lakelake
22. Lake Lakelakelake
23. Cheddar Crag
24. Cannycat Castle
25. Valley of the Giant Sequoia
26. Cheddar Springs
27. Sulfurous Swamp
28. Old Reliable Geyser
29. Vole Vale
30. Ravingrat Ravine
31. Gnat Marshes
32. Munster Highlands
33. Mousehara Desert
34. Oasis of the Sweaty Camel
35. Cabbagehead Hill
36. Rattytrap Jungle
37. Rio Mosquito

Dear mouse friends,
Thanks for reading, and farewell
till the next book.
It'll be another whisker-licking-good
adventure, and that's a promise!

Geronimo Stilton